The greatest gift you can bring to a child
is the gift of Presence.

— *Leonard Jacobson*

In Search of the Light

A Conscious Living
Publication

For Joe,
Blessings,
Leonard

For all the children in the world,
and all the parents who love and care for them.

ISBN 978-1-890580-05-6

Text copyright © 2011 by Leonard Jacobson
Illustrations copyright © 2011 by The Conscious Living Foundation

Library of Congress Control Number: 2010913658
Printed in South Korea

A CONSCIOUS LIVING PUBLICATION
La Selva Beach, CA

In Search of the Light

Written by Leonard Jacobson
Illustrated by Fiammetta Dogi

CHAPTER ONE

 here had been an eclipse of the sun. The day turned suddenly into night. The animals could not understand what had happened to the light.

A general meeting had been called to discuss the mystery.

The bells rang out calling everyone to the old banyan tree.

The first to speak was an old Billy goat who wore a long grey beard and an overcoat.

"Hear me, hear me!" he called aloud, and a silence fell upon the crowd.

"You all did see that it was dark in the middle of the day.
We, the elders, do believe that the sun had lost its way.
And if it happens again and soon, there'll be no sun, only moon.

There'll be no day, only night. It could mean the end of light."

The first to speak was an old Billy goat . . .

A panic surged through the crowd.

"Oh no!" said the doe.
"What now?" called a cow.
"I fear the very worst," a little deer loudly cursed.
"What shall we do?" asked the cockatoo.
"We're out of luck," replied a duck.
"I hate the dark!" chirped a lark.
"I hate the dark! I hate the dark!"

And then a loud voice near the rear
called out for all to hear.

"We must not accept our plight.
 We must go off in search of light."

They all agreed.

"Of course! Of course."

And all heads turned to Ned the horse.

"We'll go to the forest where no-one has been," said Ned.
"We'll follow a path which no-one has seen.
 We'll do whatever must be done to save the light, to save the sun."

"We must not fail," said Sam the snail. "I'd like to go but I'm too slow."

"It was my idea, so I'll volunteer," said Ned the horse. "I'll go of course."

"I must break this coward's habit. I guess I'll go," sighed Peter Rabbit.

"I'll join this gallant company. I'd like to make it number three," buzzed
Bert the brave little bumblebee.
"All we need is one more! Who will be number four?"

"I'll come," said Molly Mouse, stepping forward with a little bow.
"I just hope we get back somehow."

And so the fateful four were chosen.
They would leave next morning at the break of day.
Across the meadow to the forest and after that they could not say.

And so the fateful four were chosen . . .

CHAPTER TWO

Ned was the first to rise in the morning.
He hurried over to Peter's place.
As soon as Molly and Bert arrived,
they set off at a moderate pace.
Quickly they crossed the meadow.
Bert buzzed excitedly ahead. They stopped when
they reached the forest and Peter said,

"It seems as though we must go deeper
    into darkness if we are to find the light,
    for the forest is as black as the darkest night."

They stepped forward moving slowly,
unsure which way to go.
Molly lit a torch, which gave off an eerie glow.
They had not gone very far when they began to see
strange images come to life behind every tree.
There were cobwebs and spiders, snakes and rats.
Flying bats! Creatures of the night were creeping and
crawling. They thought they heard phantoms calling!
There were witches and ghosts hiding in shadows,
and they wished they were safe back in the meadow.

They stopped when they reached the forest . . .

There were witches and ghosts hiding in shadows,
and they wished they were safe back in the meadow . . .

"Is this a dream or are we awake?" said Ned.
"I wish my knees wouldn't shake! Are these things real or in the mind?
 I wonder what else we'll find?"

They stood there looking nervously around,
when suddenly they heard a whistling sound.

"Whoooo. Whooo." It sounded like the wind.

"Who are you, and what do you do?" asked the wind.

"We look for the light!" Molly said with a fright.

"Oh dear! You won't find the light here," said the wind.
"Didn't you know, this is the forest of fear!
 You must look for a friend with his own inner light.
 He'll take you to a land where nothing seems right.
 It's there you must go in search of the light, or at least you must try.
 That's all I can say. Good luck and goodbye!"

"Who are you, and what do you do?" asked the wind . . .

"It doesn't make sense," said Ned feeling tense.

"The wind cannot speak," Molly said feeling weak.

On and on they walked. No-one talked.
It seemed like they walked all day.
They often thought of turning back,
but they had lost their way.
They were lost, lost in the forest of fear.
Then, all of a sudden a flickering light came into sight
and was slowly drawing near.

"What is it?" cried Bert. "It's green and gold, with big red eyes.
  It glows as it goes and glitters as it flies. What is it?" he said with a startled cry.

"Fear not," came the answer," for I am Frederick Firefly.

"Fear not," came the answer," for I am Frederick Firefly . . .

"As you can see I have my own inner light. I've come to lead you out of the night.
  If you wish I will show you the way, but you must do exactly as I say.
  First spin and turn, jump and run."

They jumped and ran, turned and spun. Actually they had a lot of fun.

"And now, if you will, please be completely still.
  Forget everything you know. Forget where you want to go.
  Believe that you are completely free, close your eyes and count to three."

They were very bold and did exactly as they were told.
They counted. "One, two, three." It seemed like an eternity.
They opened their eyes to the strangest sight,
for they were now in a land where nothing seemed right.

They jumped and ran, turned and spun . . .

CHAPTER THREE

The grass was blue, the sky was green.
It was the strangest thing they'd ever seen.
The trees were short, the mushrooms tall.
It didn't make any sense at all.
A lion walked up and roared like a mouse
at a butterfly flying by the size of a house.
A tortoise ran by at an incredible speed
but couldn't keep up with the snail in the lead.

A lion walked up and roared like a mouse . . .

"Nothing is like it's supposed to be,"
called Bert flying in from a nearby tree.

"Let's just accept things as they are," said Ned.
"After all, we've come this far. There's a sign that says

'WRONG WAY GO BACK.'

It's my guess that that's the right track."

They set off in single file and had not gone but half a mile,
when suddenly the path divided into three, and there in the middle,
a signpost stood, clearly marked for all to see.

"To the left," it read. "The easy way. Love and joy and laughter every day."

The hard way was to the right. Pain and suffering day and night.

"To the left!" cried Peter in a very loud voice.
"The easy way! It's the obvious choice."

"No!" said Ned. "We should go to the right. We must suffer to find the light."

and there in the middle, a signpost stood, clearly marked for all to see . . .

Just then, a bird with a very large beak,
landed on the signpost and started to speak.

"Beware! This is the path of the opposites.
  Have careful regard.
  If you choose easy, it's sure to get hard.
  If you choose love, you'll also get hate.
  If you choose early, you're bound to be late.
  If you choose joy, you'll also get pain.
  If you choose sunshine, be prepared for the rain.
  If you refuse to be wrong, you'll never be right.
  If you won't accept darkness, you won't find the light."

Beware! This is the path of the opposites . . .

"What if we don't choose?" asked Molly.

"Ah, then you walk in between.
 From there, everything can be seen.
 There's no judgment. No right or wrong.
 It's the middle path you'd be walking along."

"Where does it go?" asked Bert, making sure he was heard.

"It goes no-where!" answered the bird.
"When you've been everywhere else, then you will know
 that no-where is the only place left to go.
 When you're beyond all desire and beyond all fear,
 you'll find the light. Right now. Right here."

"What if we don't choose?" asked Molly . . .

"I don't care if the bird is right!" said Ned. "I don't want to find the light.
  I'm tired of searching. I no longer care. I'm not going anywhere."

The others agreed. "There's no-where to go! No-where to go!"

Then suddenly everything started to glow and slowly turned dazzling white.

"We've found it! We've found it!" they all cried. "We've found the source of the light."

They laughed and cheered.

"The light's right here!" said Ned. "Why did we make such a fuss.
  Everything we look at comes alight, because the source of the light is in us!"

They laughed and cried and cheered and sighed.

"The source of the light is in us. The source of the light is in us."

"Our journey's over," said Molly. "Our task is done. Let's go home and tell everyone."

suddenly everything started to glow . . .

"Just one last word," said the bird, "before you return to the meadow. Remember if you're not in the center at the source of the light, then you're standing in your own shadow."

the end